CLOUD MONSTERS

To Finn,

Happy Reading!

Ellen P. Davis

10·21·22

www.mascotbooks.com

CLOUD MONSTERS

For more information, please contact:
Mascot Books
620 Herndon Parkway, Suite 320
Herndon, VA 20170
info@mascotbooks.com

Library of Congress Control Number: 2021902351

CPSIA Code: PRV0521A
ISBN-13: 978-1-64543-821-2

Printed in the United States

For my two amazing sons, Nate and Alex,
who inspire me every day.

CLOUD MONSTERS

FRANCINE PIRIANO-DAVILA

CHAPTER 1
THE PARTY

I t was the perfect spring day, bright and sunny. My younger brother Charlie and I were outside playing in our tree house. It was Charlie's eighth birthday, and we were having a big party to celebrate. All our family lived close by, so our aunts, uncles, grandparents, cousins, and friends were all coming to join the party. Charlie was so excited that he barely slept the night before.

Mom was inside making his favorite breakfast: pancakes. She wrote "Happy Birthday" on top with chocolate syrup, added whipped cream, and topped it off with a lit candle. She always loved surprising us on our birthdays. Last year, when I turned fourteen, she surprised me with a Superman balloon tied to my chair and my favorite breakfast: French toast with chocolate syrup and powdered sugar. (I thought the balloon was a little baby-ish, but I still appreciated it.)

From the treehouse, Charlie and I heard Mom call out, "Breakfast is ready!"

When Charlie saw his birthday breakfast, his eyes lit up. "Thanks, Mommy!" he said.

After he sat down, we all sang "Happy Birthday," and I told Charlie to make a wish. Charlie closed his eyes tightly and blew out the candles.

Afterwards, Charlie and I went back outside to play while our parents set up the party decorations. My dad carried some folding tables and chairs outside, and my mom set up the balloons, cups, and plates. They also put out chips, dip, and some juice boxes for the kids. We planned on ordering pizza once everyone had arrived.

The weather could not have been more perfect for an outside party—there wasn't a cloud in the sky. We had a bunch of cool outdoor activities planned for the day, like a bounce house and potato sack racing. Charlie was most excited about the face painter Mom had hired, and I was really excited about the piñata full of candy for later—a surprise for Charlie.

Soon, everyone started to arrive. Our Aunt Betsy and Uncle Ralph were the first to arrive, along with our cousins Jessica and Paul. Charlie and I liked Jessica and Paul because we were the same age and we liked playing Minecraft together. After a while, the yard was filled with our family and friends. We jumped and bounced and had so much fun. Charlie got his face painted like Spider-Man, his favorite superhero. He was enjoying his party, and I was having fun too. I loved having my friends over, because we always had a great time together. The adults seemed to be enjoying the party too. (Although I noticed some of them sneaking away to watch the football game inside.)

Finally, it was time to eat cake, so everyone ran to the table to help celebrate. Charlie had a special chair decorated with Spider-Man. His face lit up when he saw the cake. It was red and black with spider webs covering the entire cake. We sang "Happy Birthday" for the second time that day, and all of us started stuffing our faces with cake. Afterwards, Charlie opened his presents with everyone watching. He especially liked the tablet Dad and Mom got him; now he had his own—instead of having to share with me all the time.

Later, Mom put out the piñata. Charlie was so surprised, and he loved that it was in the shape of Spider-Man. He got to be the first to take a whack at it. It took about five kids swinging at the piñata before Spider-Man broke into a hundred pieces. (By the way, I was the one that finally broke it.) Candy splattered everywhere! It was a perfect day—or so we thought.

Everything was going great until, out of the blue, the sky turned completely dark. Black clouds covered the once clear blue sky. The sky was so dark and ominous—it was terrifying! Everyone thought a bad thunderstorm was getting ready to hit, so Dad told everyone to get inside.

The wind was whirling, and it quickly became very cold. Suddenly, the clouds began to spin uncontrollably. It was almost as if someone was mixing the clouds around with a big spoon. The clouds continued to spin and came dangerously close to our house. This was not a regular thunderstorm—this was something much more sinister. I was scared, but tried not to show it.

Nobody knew what was happening. The kids were screaming, and the parents were trying to calm them down. We tried to turn on the weather report, but there was no power. Dad put batteries in the radio to listen to the news, but he couldn't get it to work, so everyone went down to the basement in case the windows shattered. Charlie was crying hysterically and kept saying "I'm scared!" over and over. Mom grabbed him and held him close to calm him down. I was terrified too, but I needed to be strong for Charlie. I didn't show anyone my fear. Mom told us that this was just a bad thunderstorm and it would pass. For some reason, I didn't believe that

This was unlike any thunderstorm I had ever experienced. Where was the rain, and why was it so cold in the middle of spring? Everyone tried to remain calm, but we were losing control of the situation very quickly. What happened next was something out of a science-fiction novel—unexplainable.

CHAPTER 2
THE MONSTERS ARRIVE

Children were screaming, adults were starting to panic, and Mom and Dad were trying to keep everyone calm. We were all huddled together in the basement when, suddenly, we heard a chilling sound coming from outside the small windows above us. It sounded like a car screeching right before an accident happens. I looked out of the tiny window and saw something startling. I couldn't catch my breath, and I couldn't tear my eyes away from the window. I saw something nobody could explain: the clouds were morphing into giant shadowlike beings! They must have been fifteen feet tall each, with featureless faces. It was horrifying! They were everywhere—the cloud monsters.

The wind grew stronger, and I felt the roof trembling. Everyone was quiet, almost waiting for the wind to carry the roof away. Suddenly, it happened. The wind tore off the roof and started carrying away each level of our house. We were exposed to the elements.

Everyone now witnessed what I had seen, and they were horrified. Charlie's birthday party turned into chaos. Everyone was running in different directions trying to hide from the monsters. Mom grabbed Charlie and me and put us behind her. Charlie started screaming, "Mommy, Mommy, I'm scared!" Both of us were shaking uncontrollably. I tried to stop shaking, but I couldn't—I hoped no one would notice. Mom took us in her arms and held us tight. There was nothing left to do, and we were now at the mercy of these horrific beings.

We looked up at the blackened sky and saw thousands of flying creatures. It looked like a scene from a bad science-fiction film, but, unfortunately, this was real. Aliens were invading Earth! We were being attacked and there was nowhere to hide. I believed this was the end of the world and there was nothing we could do to stop it. At one point, I closed my eyes and prayed that this was all a dream and that I would wake up in the morning in a cold sweat.

Everyone was frozen with fear. Nobody could believe what they were seeing—it didn't seem real. All the kids were panicking and trying to run away, so the adults grabbed them and tried to shield them from the frightening giants, but there was nowhere to hide. We were completely unprotected, and the outlook of our situation was grim. There was no way out, and the flying monsters were heading right toward our house.

Without warning, a monster appeared over the house. It hovered over us, as if it was taunting us. Suddenly, another monster appeared, then another. We were surrounded, and defenseless. Everyone was trying to get away, but there was nowhere to go—the monsters were everywhere! Why were they here, and what did they want?

For a split second, I looked up at the faces of these monsters, and I was surprised by what I saw there. They didn't look menacing. Instead, I saw possible compassion in their faces. In that moment, I truly believed that they were not going to hurt us, but boy was I wrong!

They swooped down and grabbed several of my friends. My parents and I tried to help them by grabbing hold of their legs, but the monsters were too powerful. Another monster grabbed Aunt Betsy and Uncle Ralph, then Jessica and Paul. I felt helpless. I watched as these awful beasts took my family and friends.

The force of the wind made it difficult to breathe. Charlie and I were gasping for air, so Dad grabbed a blanket and put it over us to block the wind.

Mom looked at Dad and said, "Todd, what should we do?"

They both tried to come up with a plan to get everyone out of there safely. I felt like I was in a nightmare and I would wake up at any moment, but this was unimaginably real, and we needed to come up with an escape plan . . . FAST!

CHAPTER 3
ESCAPING THE MONSTERS

My Dad came up with a plan to keep everyone safe, but we had to work fast. He yelled over the piercing wind, shouting, "We need to get in our cars and drive out of here as quickly as possible! There is no other way out. We either sit and perish in the basement or try to save ourselves."

Each of us was scared, but we all agreed. There was no time to grab food and supplies. If we tried, we would risk the monsters getting to us. Everyone agreed on the escape plan and made their way to the door, sliding it open.

As if things couldn't get any worse, the oak tree that fell in our backyard was blocking our way out. "We have to try to get everyone over the tree," Dad said.

But, as we were about to help everyone over, the tree lifted off the ground and crashed into the street. Suddenly a cloud monster appeared. Startled, everyone ran in the opposite direction.

"Todd, the stairs are still there—we can get to the front of the house," Mom said. Dad told everyone to follow him to the stairs. We climbed the stairs and got out of the house.

As we ran to our cars, Charlie yelled, "Mommy, they took Grandma and Grandpa. Help them!"

Mom covered his eyes and told him we needed to keep moving. I looked back and saw my grandparents screaming for help as they were being lifted into the sky above. Through tears, Mom told Charlie and I we had to let them go.

"No!" I screamed. I ran back to try to grab them.

"Jack, come back! We can't save them now!" Mom screamed. She ran over to me and grabbed my shirt and dragged me toward the car. Tears started pouring down my face. I missed my Nana and Papi.

The next step was to get to our cars without being seen by the monsters, which seemed impossible. They watched us from above, like an eagle stalking its prey.

We were out in the open. I kept looking behind me, anticipating getting snatched by one of the monsters. The wind was so strong, we could barely walk. The adults held the children tightly against them. I grabbed onto Mom and Charlie and we began to run toward our car. There were trees down and cars toppled over. It looked like a large bomb had hit the neighborhood. I looked back and saw half our house was gone; Mom pulled me close to her and said, "Don't look back. We need to focus on getting out of here."

I tried to shield Charlie from the debris that was flying around us. At one point, I was hit in the head with a large branch and could feel blood trickling down the side of my face. It didn't even phase me. All I cared about was getting out of there without those things grabbing us.

Dad dropped the keys, but managed to grab them before they blew away. While he was fumbling with the keys, I started to shiver. The wind stopped for a moment and it suddenly became very cold. I looked up and saw a dark hand coming toward us . . . a cloud monster was now within just a few feet of us.

The monster stood there for a few moments, staring at us, almost as if it was trying to communicate.

Mom screamed, "We need to get in the car NOW! Dad opened the doors and we jumped inside. He started the car and we sped away.

We drove for about three hours until we decided to stop at a gas station. It seemed safe enough. The skies were dark, but there were no monsters in sight. Charlie was sleeping in the back seat.

Trying not to wake my little brother, I quietly faced my Dad and asked, "What are we going to do?"

He looked at me and with a broken voice said, "I don't know—let's just focus on getting gas and some food."

Dad and I went inside to grab snacks and noticed the store was totally empty. We rang the bell by the register, but no one came out to greet us. It was very odd—the monsters weren't around this area, so why was everyone gone? Suddenly, we felt an eerie presence and instead of sticking around to find out what it was, we decided to get out of there… fast. We put the money for the gas and snacks on the counter and left.

CHAPTER 4
ALIEN ENCOUNTER

We went out to the car, where Charlie was awake and hungry. We ate some snacks and sat there in silence. After a few minutes, we looked around the parking lot spotting a bright light coming from behind one of the dumpsters. I pointed to it and said, "Do you see that light?"

Dad looked at the beaming ball of light and said "Stay here, boys. I'll go check it out."

"I'll come too," I said.

Mom grabbed my arm and said, "You are not going."

Dad walked over to the dumpster and slowly looked behind it.

Mom yelled out to him, calling, "What is it?" He didn't answer.

I was getting nervous, so I called out to him again. "Dad, are you okay? What do you see?"

My dad had now disappeared behind the dumpster, and Mom started to panic, thinking the worst. She told us to stay in the car while she went to find Dad. I followed behind her and she told me to stay with Charlie. I said, "No, I want to see what's back there."

"Okay, but stay behind me," Mom replied.

We slowly peeked behind the dumpster, expecting to see Dad hurt, or worse. Instead, we beheld the most beautiful sight we had ever seen. Dad was holding a small ball of light in his arms—his face was all lit up, and he almost looked like an angel.

Stunned, I spit out, "Dad, what is that?"

My dad looked up at me with tears in his eyes. He said, "I think it's a cloud monster, but a baby one." He continued, "I think it's hurt."

The baby cloud monster was bright white with tiny arms and legs. Its face was bright white too, but it had clearly defined eyes and a mouth. I went over to take a closer look and saw a dark white fluid coming from the bottom of its leg. The baby cloud monster was wounded! I felt the need to help it, so I went closer to it. My mom told me to get back, but I did not listen, and instead continued to walk toward the small, alien creature.

"Jack, I said to get back. We don't know anything about this thing," she said.

"Mom, it's a baby and we need to help it," I softly called back.

Dad chimed in, "Abby, he's right. We need to try to help it."

We brought it to the car and put it in the back seat. Charlie was afraid of our new passenger, and he quickly moved away. Confused, he asked "What is that thing?"

"Don't worry, Charlie," I said. "We think it's friendly, and it won't hurt us."

Dad grabbed a blanket from the trunk and covered the baby monster. The baby began to cry, but it didn't sound like a typical baby cry. It sounded like the shrieking of a freight train when braking. The sound brought tears to my eyes. I thought, *This isn't a monster . . . it's a baby that needs help.*

We grabbed some gauze from the first aid kit we always kept in the car and proceeded to wrap it around the baby's leg. The baby seemed to know we were trying to help it, because it looked up at us and smiled. In the back of my mind, I thought about the baby's mother, and how she would come looking for it. I told Mom and Dad, "Maybe we should put it back by the dumpster in case its mother comes back."

Dad said, "Good idea. Once I finish wrapping its leg, I will put it back, but let's wait a while to be sure the Mom returns."

Dad lifted the helpless baby and he and I proceeded to carry it to the dumpster.

After a few seconds, we felt a cool breeze coming from above us. My Dad and I looked up and saw a giant cloud monster with its hand coming toward us. I screamed and heard Mom yelling, "Leave the baby—the mother's here!"

We put the baby carefully on the ground and ran to the car. Once we were safely inside, the giant cloud monster grabbed its baby and turned toward us. We tried to pull out of the parking lot, but our car wouldn't start.

"Todd, hurry up! It's coming for us!" Mom screamed.

The cloud monster moved closer and closer, until it was right against the window. It stared deeply into our eyes, as if trying to communicate telepathically. For a moment, I felt a sense of peace. I considered the possibility that this monster did not want to hurt us, but instead was trying to help us. I thought, how can something so frightening be good? Is it true? Could they be trying to help us and we choose not to see it because of the way they look?

As I was thinking, the car started, and we sped away. I said to Dad, "I think that was its mother."

He didn't respond. Instead, he just sat there, totally in awe of what had just transpired. Charlie was still scared, and he was silent in the back seat. I grabbed him and told him it would be okay. After about fifteen minutes, Charlie slowly said, "I think they are good."

Mom replied, "You may be right, but we just don't know what their intentions are yet."

I had this strange feeling they were trying to protect us, but why, and from what?

CHAPTER 5
BACK ON THE ROAD

We decided to get back on the road. We had no idea where we were going or what we would encounter next, but we wanted to get as far away as possible. As we drove, we couldn't help but notice that the streets were empty. There were no cars or people, and it was strangely quiet. It looked like a bomb had hit Earth. Trees were toppled over and resting on their sides, and debris from houses and stores was scattered all over the ground. Cars and trucks looked like they had been thrown around and knocked upside-down.

As we drove through these vacant streets, I thought of something that petrified me. I asked Dad, "What if the monsters were here and got to everybody already?"

He said, "Don't worry—there has to be another

explanation."

I could not think of another logical reason of why everyone was gone. *They were taken by the monsters,* I thought. *We must be next!* We continued driving, never looking back.

After driving for several minutes, we noticed something in the middle of the road. It was a little boy. Charlie said, "Mommy, that boy looks around my age. Why is he standing in the middle of the road?"

She said, "I don't know, but let's find out."

We stopped the car and got out. The boy was crying.

He said, "I lost my mommy and daddy."

As we walked over to the boy, Mom grabbed his hand to pull him over to her. Suddenly, the winds picked up, and a cloud monster swooped down from the sky and grabbed him. Mom couldn't hold on to him and she screamed, "Noooo! Leave him alone!"

The boy was screaming, too, yelling, "Help! Help me!"

There was nothing we could do. The monsters were too strong, and they eventually took the little boy away from us. Unfortunately, we could no longer save him, so we ran back to the car.

As we headed back to the car, we saw Charlie running in the opposite direction. He must have gotten scared when he saw the little boy being taken by the monsters.

"Charlie, come back here now!" Mom yelled frantically.

Mom told me to get in the car while she and my dad ran after Charlie. When they finally caught up to him, she grabbed hold of his shirt. Mom picked Charlie up and started running back to the car. That unsettling cold wind started blowing again, and we knew there wasn't much time until we saw another monster—they needed to get back to the car, now. We looked up and there they were, several cloud monsters approaching us overhead.

I screamed, "Run faster! They're getting close!"

The monsters were within a few feet of the car when Charlie and Mom fell to the ground.

I yelled, "Dad, grab Charlie!" Dad threw Charlie in the car and rushed over to grab Mom. The cloud monster was so close that we could feel its breath on our backs. Mom and Dad reached the car and got in, slamming the doors behind them and started the car as quickly as possible. The monsters were still behind us.

Charlie screamed, "Daddy, they're going to get us!"

Dad picked up the speed. We were going over 100 miles per hour now. After a few minutes, we looked behind us, and the monsters were gone. We were safe, but I knew that wouldn't last long.

CHAPTER 6
JOURNEY TO SOMEWHERE

We continued driving on this endless road to nowhere. We couldn't stop, because the monsters would find us. Where could we go from here? I was terrified of what lay ahead, and scared that my family and I would not lead normal lives again. Life as we knew it was gone, and all that was left were empty streets and vacant houses. We could see the cloud monsters in the distance, floating up in the darkened sky. They were waiting for just the right moment to take us away ... forever.

The roads were desolate, with no cars in sight, and the sky was a sinister grey color. The darkness of night would be here in a few hours. I didn't know what evils the darkness would bring, so we needed to get to safety…before blackness enveloped the Earth.

Charlie was sleeping in the back seat with Mom, and I was in the front with Dad. As we drove, we spotted another car just up ahead. I was thrilled to actually see a sign of human life! Maybe they had a plan, I hoped. I told Dad we needed to stop them, and he started honking the horn to get their attention, but they sped up. We drove until we were parallel to the passenger side window, and Dad made a gesture to open their window.

A young lady with dark hair and glasses opened the window and said, "What are you doing? Are you crazy?!"

Dad said, "No, we just haven't seen any people around, so I wanted to see where you were headed."

The lady seemed hesitant and unwilling to talk.

My dad pleaded, "Look, we're desperate."

The man in the driver's seat spoke to the woman and said, "Jo, help them."

The lady reluctantly told us they were headed to an underground cavern 400 miles north. She said it might be safe there. She pulled out a pad of paper from the glove compartment and wrote down directions for us, and after handing the paper over, they sped away. We decided to join them and started to drive the four hundred miles to the caverns.

We observed several cars on the road while driving to the caverns, and I wondered if they were heading to the same place. Charlie was awake now, and excited about going to the caverns. He asked, "Mommy, is this going to be our new home?"

Mom was stumped and didn't know how to answer that, so she looked at the map we keep in the car and said, "I don't know, sweetie. It will be for a while. We are about three hundred and fifty miles out."

I was eager to get there. I hoped we would be safe there and the monsters would never be able to get to us again.

We decided to stop at a grocery store on the way so we could bring some food to the caverns: snacks, water, and canned goods. Charlie and I waited in the car with Mom while Dad went to get the stuff. Charlie and I were staring at the window at the near-empty parking lot. Charlie was traumatized by the day's events, but there was nothing I could do to make it better for him, even though I was his big brother. I felt totally powerless. I was mentally and physically exhausted. I leaned my head against the window and closed my eyes, hoping when I woke up, this would all turn out to have been a bad dream.

I watched through the car window as Dad grabbed a cart and walked into the store. Later, Dad told us about the strange woman he met in the store. He said the store was completely empty—there wasn't a soul in sight. He carried on with his shopping, when he noticed a little old woman standing at the end of the aisle. She was wearing a blue house dress with dirty black boots. She had on a hat with a black veil covering her face. As he walked past her, he heard, "Leave now."

He turned around and said, "Excuse me?"

She said, "You are in danger; Leave now, or you will never get out alive."

Dad thought she was just a crazy old woman and ignored her. He was just about to walk away when she started to yell, "HEY, DIDN'T YOU HEAR ME? GET OUT, OR YOU WILL DIE!"

He was so scared by this outburst that he dropped the cans on the floor and ran.

I must admit, after hearing his story, I was pretty freaked out!

As we sat waiting for Dad, we listened to the storm brewing outside. Leaves rustled, and the branches began falling to the ground. The cold air crept through the open window, and I said, "This doesn't look good. We have to get out of here." Charlie and my mom agreed. Mom drove the car to the front of the store and honked. Dad heard and, thinking we were in trouble, grabbed some chips and water on the way out and hurried to the car. He quickly threw the stuff in the trunk, and we drove out of the parking lot.

We had managed to dodge the aliens again, but for how long?

CHAPTER 7
JOURNEY TO THE CAVERNS

We still had several hundred miles of driving before we reached the caverns when Mom suggested, "Let's play a game."

I think she wanted to get our minds off what was happening, so we played the Name Game.

"Okay, the first animal is a pig." Mom called.

"I got it—goose!" Charlie shouted. "Daddy, you're next."

"How about an elephant?" he said.

We were having a great time, and it almost seemed like we were are on a normal road trip.

"Jack, you're next!" Charlie said.

"Tiger—groooowlll," I kidded.

Everyone laughed.

"I'm next," Charlie said. "I've got a good one: lion. ROAR!"

"You're supposed to come up with an animal that starts with an 'R,' stupid," I said.

"Mommy, Jack called me a bad name!" Charlie whined.

Usually, Mom would get annoyed at the two of us arguing, but right now it was music to her ears. It made the day seem just a little bit more normal.

A few miles down the road, we spotted a group of horses blocking the interstate. There must have been hundreds of them. They were standing in the middle of the interstate, looking up . . . almost like they were waiting for something. We were all confused.

"Why are they standing in the middle of road?" Dad wondered aloud. He was starting to get frustrated. He screamed out the window, "Get out of the road!"

Mom honked the horn continuously as we watched from a distance. The horses did not budge. It's like they were in a trance. They stubbornly stood there and did not move. The entire road was blocked, so we couldn't even get around them. Mom honked again. There was no response. We would have to wait until they were ready to move.

Suddenly, there was that familiar wind. Mom said, "Oh no, they're here . . . and they're going to take the horses!"

We looked up, and there they were—the monsters! Mom turned the car around and sped off. Still looking back, I said, "Huh. The horses aren't trying to get away." It was strange. Why would the horses let the monsters capture them? It didn't make any sense.

After driving about two miles, we again encountered another group of animals. This time, there were hundreds of them: racoons, squirrels, opossums, and any other animal you could think of. Again, they stood in the middle of the road, waiting. It was bizarre seeing them all together in a group. They were looking up at the sky, focusing intently.

Dad said, "We'd better get out of here; I bet they will be here soon."

I said, "We can't go back, the monsters are there."

Dad responded that he thought the animals and monsters would be gone, so it would be okay to go back.

We drove about two miles in the opposite

direction, returning to the area where the horses had once stood. Everything was quiet now—the monsters and horses were gone. We doubled back and passed by the part of the road where the other animals had stood, and they were all gone too. It was like they had all vanished into thin air. I wondered if they knew something that we didn't. They say animals have a sixth sense about these things.

Charlie was concerned about the animals and worried that they were hurt. He asked, "Mommy, are the animals okay?"

He had always loved animals, so I knew he was upset about the monsters taking them away. Mom told him they were probably fine, and not to worry. I started thinking and noticed that I hadn't even seen a squirrel on the side of the road, or a bird flying in the trees next to the road, in hours. I realized that there were no birds, squirrels, or animals of any kind left on Earth. Had they all gone with the monsters willingly, like the horses? Animals usually run away from danger, but they didn't run. It's almost as if they were expecting them, or had been waiting to be taken by the monsters.

We had a few hours left in the car before we reached the caverns, so we all crossed our fingers that we wouldn't encounter any horses or racoons or anything else that could get in our way. This had not been an easy journey and all of us were mentally exhausted, so we need some good luck to come our way. Eventually, we did have a bit of good luck . . . sort of.

CHAPTER 8
AN UNEXPECTED SURPRISE

We were about halfway to the caverns when we spotted a truck on the side of the road. As Charlie's face lit up, I yelled, "Hey, that's an ice cream truck! Let's go check it out!"

We pulled over behind the truck and got out. "Be careful," warned Dad with a concerned voice.

We walked over to the window slowly, but there was no one in the truck.

Mom said, "Well, let's get some ice cream. We deserve it!" She opened the door and hopped up into the truck, opening the freezer.

Charlie started jumping up and down and gave Mom his order, calling out, "I will have a Spider-Man popsicle!"

"Give me an ice cream sandwich, please," I said, with excitement in my voice.

"Okay, coming right up," Mom replied.

As Charlie and I peeked into the truck, we heard a strange but familiar noise coming from underneath the counter: the sound of a small freight train coming to a stop. Suddenly, a small cloud monster popped out and jumped in front of my mom. Thinking fast, I opened the door to the truck and blocked my mom from the monster. The monster inched closer to me, and I jumped back, but I wasn't afraid. It looked young, maybe around the same age as Charlie. I somehow knew it wouldn't harm me—it almost seemed scared of me.

"What's going on in there? Are you okay?" Dad asked.

Mom said, "We're fine—just give us a few minutes."

I tried to communicate with the monster, looking directly into its eyes and asking, "What do you want from us?"

Mom tried to pull me away, but I kept moving closer. The monster didn't answer. I asked again, "What do you want?"

The monster stared deeply into my eyes and stuck out its hand, intending for me to grab it. I was hesitant, but decided to do it. Mom tried to stop me from grabbing its hand, but I said, "Mom, don't worry. I think he is trying to tell us something."

She backed off and let me touch its hand, but still held onto my other arm, in case she needed to pull me away. I touched its hand and closed my eyes, and a surge of electricity ran through my body. I felt myself take a step backwards. After the initial shock of the cloud monster's touch, I was bombarded with images of Earth, of the cloud monsters surrounding us, of large black monster-like beings and of an explosion. Overwhelmed, I let go of its hand and opened my eyes. The young cloud monster was gone. It had been trying to tell me something, but what? Confused, I wanted to ask it more questions. *What does this all mean?* I thought. *Are the cloud monsters good or evil?*

Dad jumped into the ice cream truck and said, "Are you okay? I saw a cloud monster fly out of here."

I said, "Dad, I don't believe they are trying to hurt us."

He looked puzzled. "What?! They are trying to

capture us, and they took away our family and friends! Everyone on Earth is practically gone, and you think these things are good?"

I said, "I know it sounds crazy, Dad, but I think the monster in the truck was trying to warn me of something."

Frustrated, he started to walk away.

"Where are you going?" I asked.

"We'd better get back on the road. Let's grab our ice cream and head out," he said.

While driving to the caverns, I thought about the visions, and about what Dad had said about the monsters. I want to believe these monsters were good, but I have to assume otherwise. I hoped Dad was wrong, but, until we find out more answers, I guess we need to keep moving.

CHAPTER 9
WE'VE BEEN CAUGHT

After a couple hours on the road, Charlie needed to go to the bathroom, so we pulled over. Dad took Charlie while Mom and I waited in the car. It was quiet . . . too quiet. The silence was unsettling. I just wanted Dad and Charlie to come back to the car so we could get out of there.

Suddenly, I felt the wind pick up through the open window and heard a disturbing sound. I looked up at the sky and saw a now-familiar sight: the clouds were turning into monsters, and these ones looked bigger and more sinister than before. Mom screamed, "Todd, let's go! They're back!"

Dad ran back with Charlie and put him in the car. Charlie was crying. We tried to get away, but the monsters were right behind us. They were everywhere. There was no escape. I looked behind us and saw one of them getting ready to grab the car. I said, "Mom, speed up! They're right behind us!"

She said, "I am going as fast as I can, but they're too quick! I can't lose them!"

Suddenly, we felt the car being lifted off the ground. I jumped in the back seat and grabbed Charlie, holding him tight. I looked out the car window and saw nothing but clouds and blue sky. I felt like I was losing control.

The sky outside started to get very dark—we were now surrounded by smoke! I couldn't see anything, and I knew there was nothing more we could do to defend ourselves. We were at the mercy of these monstrous beings.

After a few minutes the smoke cleared, and we looked out the window. Charlie asked, "Where are we?"

It was dark, so I couldn't tell. My family and I were too scared to get out of the car, so we just sat there and waited. Eventually, something did happen—we felt the car being lifted again. The doors opened and the car started to gently shake from side to side. There was nothing to hold onto, so we had no choice but to jump from the car with no knowledge of where we would land. As we prepared to jump, Dad told me and Charlie to grab hold of him and Mom and hold on tight. Suddenly, the force of the shaking became too great to control our movements, and before we had a chance to grab on to them, we fell out. Mom screamed "Jack, Charlie—NO!"

After falling a few feet, Charlie and I landed on a soft, sticky ground. I heard Mom scream "Jack, Charlie, are you alright?"

I didn't answer at first because I was too disoriented from the fall and from not knowing where I was. I could hear Charlie right beside me, crying. I Tried to lift my feet up to go and comfort him, but I couldn't move. We were trapped in the sticky substance!

Again, Mom yelled out, "Jack and Charlie, answer me if you're okay!"

Recovering from the jump, I said, "We're fine, Mom—just stuck in something sticky, so we can't move."

Reassured, Mom and Dad jumped out of the car

and landed right beside us. After a few minutes of struggling to move our feet, we managed to pull ourselves free.

"Thank goodness you boys are okay," Mom said.

I think she hugged us for several minutes before finally letting go.

"Don't worry, we're okay," I replied.

We were all fine and unharmed. We just didn't know where we were.

CHAPTER 10
WHERE ARE WE?

It was cold and dark. We were all scared, and I was still in shock and disbelief, but we started to explore our surroundings. Aside from the track lighting on the ground, it was pitch black and we couldn't see anything. Dad carried Charlie so he wouldn't get lost, and Mom and I walked behind. She told me to stay close, saying, "I don't want to lose you again."

I could hear Charlie crying softly in the background. Dad softly told him not to worry, that we will find a way out of here. Somehow, though, I knew that we would never leave.

I felt around for anything that would tell us where we were. I swept my hand across what I thought was a wall and felt a hard substance, like metal—a windowpane? After some exploring, I discovered that there were windows every few feet, and I found something that felt like a small television. Out of the darkness, I called, "Dad, Mom, look at this."

Dad ran over and started feeling around for a power button, but he couldn't locate it. Suddenly, the screen turned bright blue. Then, a picture started to appear.

"What is that?" Dad wondered aloud.

The video showed giant, foul-looking beings dressed in black from head to toe. They had enormous creepy black eyes and no mouths, and multiple limbs with claws the size of a small car. They looked like pure evil. Mom told us to cover our eyes.

"Mom, I saw those things before, remember? The cloud monster in the ice cream truck showed me images of . . ." I couldn't finish. I was so scared of what I had just seen; I just wanted to melt in my mom's arms and never let go.

I was confused. Were there two species of monsters, or was there one species that could morph into anything they wanted? Suddenly, I had a terrifying thought. I whispered to Dad so Charlie wouldn't hear, saying, "Are those the things that took us?"

Dad said, "I don't know. The things that captured us looked different."

We were baffled by what we saw and didn't know what to think. Even though this was terrifying, we decided to move on from the video playing on the TV and focus on getting out of there. We didn't want to scare Charlie (although, to be honest, I was scared enough for all of us).

We continued walking down this dark, never-ending hallway until we heard Dad say, "Look! Over here."

We followed the sound of his voice.

"I think it's a bridge of some sort," he continued. We carefully went to walk across the bridge-like walkway. It had a railing and felt solid enough to walk on. While walking across, I was reminded of the time when I was eight, and we went on a trip to San Francisco and walked over the Golden Gate Bridge. I would have given anything to be there again.

While we walked over the bridge, the sound of our footsteps echoed through the room. It almost seemed like we were suspended over a bottomless pit. Mom and Dad kept us close because they didn't know if the bridge would eventually end, dropping us in the dark abyss.

We kept hearing voices, but it was so dark that we couldn't see where they were coming from. I kept thinking something would grab me from behind and throw me over the railing. Mom was scared, too, holding on to Charlie and me so tightly that we could barely breathe.

After walking for about fifteen minutes, the bridge finally ended. Our voices were echoing even louder now, so it seemed like we were in a larger area this time. We felt around again to find out any clues to where we were. The walls were smooth and hard, and the ground was moving slowly beneath our feet. Unsteady, we tried to keep our balance. It was like walking on a dock when the water is a little too rough.

Suddenly, the floor became very narrow and, paired with the unsteadiness, we found it difficult to walk. It seemed like we were on another bridge, but this was much wobblier than the first one. There was no railing to hold on to, so we had to walk slowly across, stopping every few seconds to catch our balance.

Suddenly, Charlie started to scream, "Help, Mommy, I can't hold on anymore!"

When we rushed over to him, Dad was trying to pull him up, and Charlie's hands were holding on to the edge of the bridge, his body dangling into the open air.

"Help me get him up!" Dad yelled.

We managed to pull him up to safety. He was shaken up, but otherwise okay.

Mom said, "Thank goodness you're alright! We almost lost you!"

Charlie tried to be brave and said, "I'm okay, Mommy. Don't worry." Despite his words, he still clung tight to our mother, sniffling a little bit.

We managed to maintain our balance and continued on to solid ground.

Charlie was tired, so we decided to stop and rest for a while.

"I'm thirsty," he said.

"I know, honey. We'll try to find you some water," Mom said.

Dad grabbed Mom's hand and said, "We will get through this."

I wanted to believe that, but I had my doubts. I kept thinking about those things we saw on the TV and wondering if this was their ship. They did not seem like friendly monsters, so their intentions must have been to harm us. I was worried for my family and what would happen to us. In my mind, I knew we would never step foot on Earth again.

Again, we started hearing voices. Where are they coming from?

CHAPTER 11
WHEN THE LIGHTS TURNED ON

We continued to walk until something hard stopped us. It was like hitting a glass wall, and we couldn't go any further. We turned around to try and go back, but we were surrounded by this glass wall. We were trapped. I started to rethink the fact that these monsters might be good. If they were decent, why would they scare us like this? Why wouldn't they tell us what's going on?

Charlie asked, "What did we hit?"

"I don't know, honey," Mom said.

I had a feeling we were going to find out very soon. We sat in this glass cage for what seemed like hours until, suddenly, it became very bright. There was so much light that we could barely see, and we could hear people screaming in the background. Scared, Mom told us to close our eyes. She grabbed on to us and held us tight. What was happening?

Eventually, the intense light dimmed, and we could finally see where we were: We were in a small glass enclosure with a large black window. There were hundreds of people around us, encased in their own enclosures—the source of the voices we heard in the background. Inside of our own glass box, our bodies started floating upward. When we finally hit the ceiling, we were suspended about ten feet above the ground. Charlie started to cry, and Mom and Dad got underneath us in case we suddenly fell. While Mom was trying to calm down Charlie, I looked around and noticed we were surrounded by cloud monsters. There must have been hundreds of them, all staring at us with sorrow on their faces. Judging from their expressions, I knew we were in trouble.

The black window in our glass room slowly opened, and our bodies gently descended back down to the floor of our glass enclosure. With the lights on and the window open, we finally knew exactly where we were: a spaceship. From the window, we could see the Earth was directly below us. The other families in their own enclosures were watching with amazement and fright.

I turned to Dad and said, "Why are we here? What do they want with us?"

He did not answer. Instead, he just looked at me with an expression of dread on his face. Charlie was holding on to me so tightly that I thought I was going to faint.

Dad told us that even though he didn't know what was happening, he wouldn't let anything happen to us. Seeing the fear in his eyes made me feel scared and angry at the same time. How could these things do this to us? I kept telling myself that they must have a good reason, but looking at the terror in my parents' and my brother's eyes, I couldn't think of one.

Seeing Earth from this distance was both majestic and terrifying at the same time. Yesterday, we were at a party singing "Happy Birthday," and now we were on a spaceship looking down at Earth. It was surreal. I thought this was the sort of thing that only happened in science-fiction movies, but this was real life.

CHAPTER 12
THE EXPLANATION

One of the cloud monsters started speaking. He was smaller than the others, but had a commanding voice.

He said, "My name is Saitchu. I am from the planet Zelia. Welcome to our ship. We are not going to harm you. We want to protect you."

I felt a sense of relief that they would not harm us, but I still wondered why we needed protection. Fortunately, I didn't need to wait long for the answer. This time, Saitchu did not speak, but instead pointed at Earth. Within seconds, Earth exploded! Everyone on the ship started to scream, and Charlie hid behind Mom, shaking uncontrollably. We all watched Earth shatter into a million pieces, large and small rocks floating everywhere. I felt an overwhelming feeling of grief and anger. Our planet was gone. Our home was gone.

The monster spoke again, now with sorrow in his voice. "I'm sorry you had to watch your home get destroyed. Please let me explain."

He went on to say that aliens from the planet Vultor were planning our demise for a long time. They had destroyed thousands of planets within the past five thousand years, and we were their latest victims. The Vultans wanted to be the only beings in the universe, and had already wiped out several galaxies. The cloud monsters knew about their plan to destroy Earth, so they decided to help us. They did not want to see another planet destroyed and lives lost.

Saitchu went on to say, "We are in the process of building a bomb to destroy their planet so that we can put a stop to the endless loss of life in our universe. Until then, we will try to save the lives of any beings in their path. We have a spy on the planet Vultor to provide any information on their next move, so we can be one step ahead of them at all times.

Listening to Saitchu speak, I realized that the

Vultans were the things we saw on the television. I was thankful we weren't in the hands of those monsters. Seeing Earth blow up before my eyes had been terrible and indescribable. I was angry and saddened by the prospect of never seeing Earth again, but at the same time, I was grateful that we were still alive and safe.

Everyone on the spaceship was listening intently and trying to absorb the information Saitchu was relaying to them, while I was still trying to grasp the magnitude of the situation. Was this really happening? Were we actually on an alien spaceship on our way to a distant planet? I still feel like I will wake up from this nightmare and find myself in my own bed in my home on Earth.

Saitchu continued, saying that the Zelians had several planets in their galaxy on which they could house the many billions of people they were rescuing. Their plan was to rescue as many beings as possible and get them to safety. He said they had thousands of ships to transport everyone. He apologized for frightening us, but let us know that it had been the only way to get us on their ship quickly. "This rescue mission was a success. Our advanced thermal imaging equipment detects heat from all living things, so we are confident that we saved every human being and every single animal on Earth. You will now begin your new lives on our planet," Saitchu explained. He said, "I know this is a scary time for all of you, but I want to reassure you, we will do our best to make you feel as comfortable as possible and we will try to recreate your life on Earth as it was before you left."

Saitchu said that they would be taking us to their planet, Zelia, to live, and that we didn't need to worry about the Vultans anymore. We would be traveling through a wormhole which would take us trillions of light years away. He said that we would be safe there until the Vultans planet is destroyed.

I trusted Saitchu, and truly wanted to believe that we can still lead normal lives, but I wondered how that was possible when we would be living in a galaxy trillions of miles away from our home! I thought about the little café Mom and Dad owned on Earth, wondering, *Will they still be able to own a restaurant on this new planet? How will we go to school? Where will we live?* I had so many unanswered questions, but I guessed we would have to wait until we arrived at our new home to find out the answers.

The ship was quiet despite the countless people on the spacecraft. Everyone was still in shock and disbelief. Everything happened so fast that there was no time to prepare. I was still trying to grasp the idea of living on another planet. We didn't know whether to cry or to smile and be thankful we were still alive. I looked at my family and felt a sense of relief. My parents and little brother were alive, and that's all that mattered.

CHAPTER 13
JOURNEY TO ZELIA

We had been on the spaceship for just over two months and were adjusting quite well to our new surroundings. The Zelians, formerly known as the cloud monsters, were treating everyone well. My family even had our own suite on the spaceship with a little kitchen and bathroom. Charlie and I had a room with bunk beds, which Charlie absolutely loved because he could spend more time with me. The Zelians even supplied toys for Charlie right after we arrived, and he had been playing with them happily for the last two months. They had given me drawing paper and canvases with markers and paint brushes because they knew I loved art. Unbelievably, we were even able to play Minecraft on the ship! I don't know how the cloud monsters were able to do that, but I wasn't complaining. We were doing very well, considering what we had been through the past couple months. We even got to see Aunt Betsy and Uncle Paul every day, along with our cousins. They lived two floors below us. I think it helped Charlie and I to be with our cousins again.

We had an endless supply of food, which we got delivered to our room every week. Apparently, the cloud monsters were able to bring food from Earth to help feed us on the journey to their planet. Heshion, our delivery man, always brought a special treat for us: candy and LEGOS.

There was an activity room on each floor with tons of games, like ping pong, air hockey, pool and endless others. We were there every day playing with humans and aliens alike. Charlie and I made friends with a few of the boy Zelians. They were pretty cool, even though they were twice our size!

We all grew to like the Zelians. They were gentle and kind, and they always made sure we were okay. I even became friends with a Zelian boy named Jalu. I would tell him about Earth and he would fill me in on his planet. It's hard to believe that, just a few months before, we thought the Zelians were evil monsters. Now I felt horrible for even thinking that way, but because of the way they appeared to us so suddenly and terribly on planet Earth, there had been no other way to think.

Saitchu said that we should arrive on planet Zelia in a few months, and we would finally get to see our new home. He said that when we arrive, we would have a Zelian helping us every step of the way. They would find us a house and get us situated in our new home. I still had a lot of questions concerning our new home, but Saitchu scheduled a meeting later that day to update us on the situation and answer any questions or concerns we might have had.

Saitchu announced that we would be traveling through the wormhole in a few days, so we needed to be prepared. He told us what to expect and how to handle the transition, informing us that the ship would be passing through the wormhole at a speed of 150,000 miles per second. Even though the ship was well-equipped to handle the pressure of the wormhole's gravitational pull, he let us know that we would have aftereffects from the immense pressure put on our bodies. Due to the prolonged exposure and speed at which we will be traveling, these aftereffects would include headaches and nausea that would pass after a few weeks. We were instructed to remain in our rooms with seatbelts on for protection, and the crew would let us know when it is safe to leave our seats—the journey to their galaxy would only take a matter of hours.

Saitchu mentioned something else which disturbed everyone on the ship and caused a bit of hysteria. Over the loudspeaker, he announced, "We will be going through a time warp, so after passing through the wormhole, it will be ten years in the future."

After hearing this, I admit I was a bit freaked out, as was everyone else on the ship. I thought, *What does this mean? Will I be ten years older when we get there? Or twenty-four years old?*

After some of us voiced concerns, Saitchu responded, "Don't worry, you all will age at an imperceptible rate, so you will not notice any change in your bodies or appearances."

I had my doubts. I was afraid to go so far away from our home. This was a dangerous journey, and I was terrified of what was to come. I'd seen movies about traveling through wormholes to distant galaxies, but never actually thought I would be going through one myself. We would be trillions of light years away from our home! I still couldn't believe we were on an alien ship headed to a galaxy ten years in the future. It still didn't seem real to me.

CHAPTER 14
ALL ABOUT PLANET ZELIA

One day, Saitchu called everyone to the main section of the ship for a meeting. He said "I have received many questions about life on planet Zelia, and I will try to give detailed information about our planet. First, I want to address the language issue. I have been asked how we know the language of the Earthlings. As a matter of fact, we have been speaking our native tongue. It is actually you who know the language of the Zelians. When you first arrived on our ship, we taught you our language through thought transference, so you are indeed speaking and communicating in Zelian, and have been this whole time.

Everyone was dumbfounded. I, for one, was amazed at this revelation. Charlie said, "We are actually speaking Zelian? How cool!"

Saitchu continued, "We have two suns and five moons. There are no seasons and it is hot most of the time. Most of the planet is desert, but we do have beautiful places to visit." He mentioned the mountains that covered half their planet. "They are quite beautiful," he said.

"I have received many questions regarding schooling for the children, and if the adults will be able to work. Let me assure you that the Zelians have already started building schools for your children. Just like on Earth, you will have human teachers to provide for your children's educational needs. We will provide extra instruction from our fellow Zelians to teach the children about the history of the Zelians and our way of life.

"The question I have been asked the most is 'Where will we live?' Zelians do not live in the typical houses you're used to on Earth. We live in caves, where it's cooler, so we will be building above ground cave-like structures for the humans. They will have kitchens, bathrooms, and windows. You can even have a garden and grow all the plants native to our planet, if you'd like. You will have all of the comforts you had on Earth, just in a different way. Also, our planet is rich in oxygen, so there is no need to live in a bubble or wear a space suit." There were sighs of relief across the entire ship.

Saitchu continued, "Many Earthlings had questions about the Zelian way of life: Do we eat? Do we work and make money? The answer is no. We do not eat like humans. Zelians receive nourishment from the many trees native to our planet. The Chilia and Koyan trees are our main source of food. We understand the human body has a different molecular structure then our bodies, so we will be able to provide an abundance of Earth food to help you survive. We will supply greenhouses to grow vegetables and fruits for human consumption. With our advanced technology, we can grow crops full of all the necessary building blocks for humans to survive on our planet. You will eat just as you ate on Earth."

Saitchu said there would be a home for all of Earth's animals as well. He mentioned a neighboring planet rich in soil, which was much smaller than Zelia, but big enough to house all of Earth's forest creatures.

The Zelians had already planted seeds from Earth, and there was now an abundance of trees. They had even built a habitat for the cold-weather animals, like polar bears and penguins, to live in. Our neighbor planet, Cotu, was further away from our suns and mostly composed of water, so the Zelians would house the whales, dolphins and all of Earth's aquatic wildlife there. I thought, *Wow, the Zelians have thought of everything. They were well-prepared for our arrival for a long time.*

Saitchu went on to say, "To answer the question about money and if the Zelians work for a living—the answer is no. The Zelians work together as a free society. We are all family, and we help each other. We do not possess material objects, so there is no need for money in our world. We work hard to keep our planet safe from any potential threats from outside our galaxy. We realize humans will need to adjust to this new way of life, but we will make this transition as easy as possible for you. We will provide most of the luxuries you had on Earth, such as grocery stores, restaurants, and even playgrounds for the younger Earthlings, but there will be no payment required for any of those services. We will all work together to ensure everything is running smoothly. All that we ask is that you follow our rules and respect our wishes. We are free of violence and crime, so we will not tolerate any humans partaking in such offenses. We wish to live a peaceful existence and hope you will help maintain the harmony of our planet. If anyone breaks these rules, they will be exiled to our neighboring planet Bacu, where it is isolated and cold; these offenders will live out the rest of their lives there."

Saitchu concluded his speech with, "Thank you, Earthlings. I hope I did not leave any questions unanswered. I hope that one day you will consider our planet your own. Peace be with you all."

It would be a huge adjustment for us, but I knew that we would be happy in the end, considering the alternative. We could have been on Earth when it exploded into a million pieces, and we had been so close to all our lives ending that way. We were so lucky the Zelians cared enough to save us from death, and we owed them so much. They may look scary and intimidating, but inside they were the most beautiful, compassionate, and caring spirits I had ever encountered.

CHAPTER 15
A NEW LIFE

Five years have passed since we've been living on planet Zelia. Charlie is in seventh grade, and I am in my third year of college. We have many friends, alien and human alike. Mom and Dad opened their own restaurant, which they appropriately named "The Cloud Tavern." We all learned greatly from this experience. Most importantly, we learned not to judge people by appearances. Even though the cloud monsters looked frightening in the beginning, they are actually good beings who wanted to help us. They are no longer known among Earthlings as "the cloud monsters." Instead, we consider them our friends. We will be forever grateful to them for saving our lives. The Zelians were willing to share their planet with humans and sacrifice themselves for our happiness. I believe we all learned a huge lesson from all of this—don't judge a book by its cover. The book made be old and torn from the outside, but the inside can have the most beautiful words ever written. That's what the Zelians are—beautiful inside and out.

We are living a peaceful existence and could not be happier with our lives. The Earth is gone, but we were able to start a new life in this world: an alien world.

ABOUT THE AUTHOR

Francine Piriano-Davila grew up reading science fiction, and she has always loved the genre. She was inspired to write *Cloud Monsters* by her hope to get books in kids' hands, and that they'd be drawn in by the fantastic worlds that first attracted her to reading. Francine lives in Springfield, Virginia, with her husband, Pete, and her two energetic boys, Nate and Alex, along with their cat, Benjamin. This is her first book.

FRANCINE PIRIANO-DAVILA

CLOUD MONSTERS

CLOUD MONSTERS

FRANCINE PIRIANO-DAVILA